PUFFIN BOOKS

More of
Milly -Molly -Mandy

Joyce Lankester Brisley (1896–1978) wrote and drew books from an early age; she had her first fairy story published in a children's paper at the age of thirteen. She studied at art school and, when she was twenty, had pictures hung in the Royal Academy. However, she enjoyed writing and illustrating stories best, and the Milly-Molly-Mandy series deservedly became her most well-loved and famous creation, adored by little girls everywhere, even now more than eighty years after they were first written.

More of
Milly -Molly -Mandy

Joyce Lankester Brisley

PUFFIN

PUFFIN BOOKS

Published by the Penguin Group
Penguin Books Ltd, 80 Strand, London WC2R ORL, England
Penguin Group (USA) Inc., 375 Hudson Street, New York, New York 10014, USA
Penguin Group (Canada), 90 Eglinton Avenue East, Suite 700, Toronto, Ontario, Canada M4P 2Y3
(a division of Pearson Penguin Canada Inc.)
Penguin Ireland, 25 St Stephen's Green, Dublin 2, Ireland (a division of Penguin Books Ltd)
Penguin Group (Australia), 250 Camberwell Road, Camberwell, Victoria 3124, Australia
(a division of Pearson Australia Group Pty Ltd)
Penguin Books India Pvt Ltd, 11 Community Centre, Panchsheel Park, New Delhi – 110 017, India
Penguin Group (NZ), 67 Apollo Drive, Rosedale, North Shore 0632, New Zealand
(a division of Pearson New Zealand Ltd)
Penguin Books (South Africa) (Pty) Ltd, 24 Sturdee Avenue, Rosebank, Johannesburg 2196, South Africa

Penguin Books Ltd, Registered Offices: 80 Strand, London WC2R ORL, England

puffinbooks.com

First published by George G. Harrap 1929
Published in Puffin Books 1972
This edition produced for The Book People Ltd,
Hall Wood Avenue, Haydock, St Helens, WA11 9UL

1

Set in Monotype Baskerville
Made and printed in England by Clays Ltd, St Ives plc

The stories and most of the drawings first appeared in the Children's Page of the
Christian Science Monitor, *and I am very grateful for*
permission to reprint them here.
J. L. B.

British Library Cataloguing in Publication Data
A CIP catalogue record for this book is available from the British Library

ISBN: 978-0-141-33640-4

www.greenpenguin.co.uk

Mixed Sources
Product group from well-managed
forests and other controlled sources
www.fsc.org Cert no. SA-COC-1592
© 1996 Forest Stewardship Council
FSC

Penguin Books is committed to a sustainable future
for our business, our readers and our planet.
The book in your hands is made from paper
certified by the Forest Stewardship Council.

Contents

1. Milly-Molly-Mandy Gets Up Early 9
2. Milly-Molly-Mandy Has a Surprise 17
3. Milly-Molly-Mandy Gets Up a Tree 25
4. Milly-Molly-Mandy Goes to a Concert 33
5. Milly-Molly-Mandy Has her Photo Taken 41
6. Milly-Molly-Mandy Goes to the Pictures 50
7. Milly-Molly-Mandy Goes for a Picnic 58
8. Milly-Molly-Mandy Looks for a Name 66
9. Milly-Molly-Mandy Gets Locked In 75
10. Milly-Molly-Mandy's Mother Goes Away 85
11. Milly-Molly-Mandy Goes to the Sea 94
12. Milly-Molly-Mandy Finds a Nest 103
13. Milly-Molly-Mandy Has Friends 111

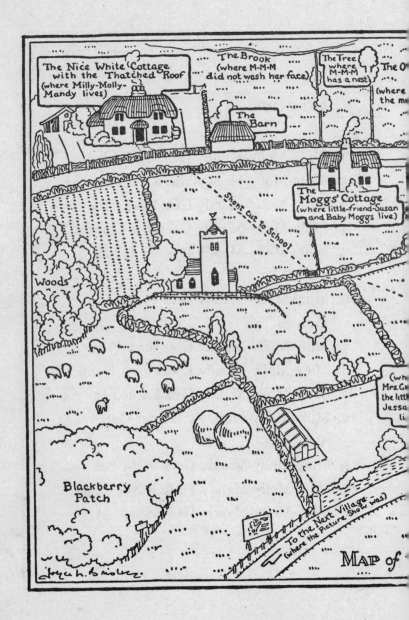

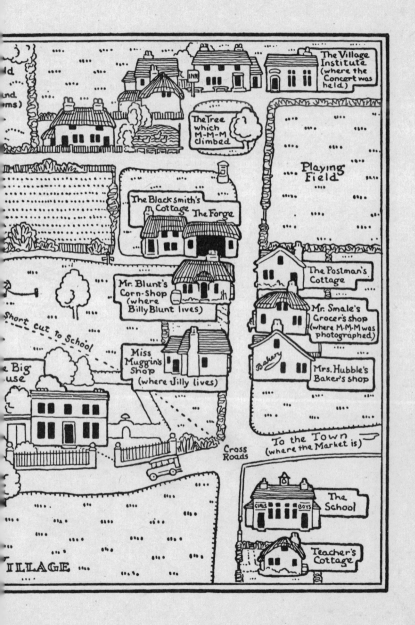

The Village
Institute
(where the
Concert was
held)

The Tree
which
M-M-M
climbed

Playing
Field

The Blacksmith's
Cottage   The Forge

The Postman's
Cottage

Mr. Blunt's
Corn-Shop
(where
Billy Blunt lives)

Mr. Smale's
Grocer's shop
(where M-M-M was
photographed)

Short cut to School

Miss
Muggin's
Shop
(where Jilly lives)

Bakery

Mrs. Hubble's
Baker's shop

e Big
use

To the Town
(where the Market is)

Cross
Roads

GIRLS   BOYS

The
School

Teacher's
Cottage

ILLAGE

1. Milly-Molly-Mandy Gets Up Early

Once upon a time, one beautiful summer morning, Milly-Molly-Mandy woke up very early.

She knew it was very early, because Father and Mother were not moving (Milly-Molly-Mandy's cot-bed was in one corner of Father's and Mother's room). And she knew it was a beautiful summer morning, because the cracks around the window-blinds were so bright she could hardly look at them.

Milly-Molly-Mandy (whose full name was really Millicent Margaret Amanda) knelt up on the foot of her cot-bed and softly lifted one corner of the blind, and peeped out.

And it was the most beautiful, quiet summer morning that ever was.

The doves in the dove-cote were saying '*Coo-roo-o-o!*' to each other, in a soft, lazy sort of way; and the hens round the hen-house in the field were saying '*Ker-ruk-ruk!*' to each other, in a soft, busy sort of way; and Old Marmaduke the cock was yelling '*Doodle-doo!*' to everybody, at the top of his voice, only it sounded soft because he was right the other side of the barn.

'Well!' said Milly-Molly-Mandy to herself. 'It's much too beautiful a morning to stay in bed till breakfast-time. I think I'll get up very, very quietly, so's not to wake Father and Mother.'

So Milly-Molly-Mandy slid out of bed very, very quietly, and she slid into her socks, and into her clothes as far as her petticoat.

And then she crept to the wash-stand, but she didn't think she could manage the big water-jug without waking Father and Mother. So she took up her shoes and her pink-striped cotton frock, and she creepy-crept to the door and opened it, only making just one tiny little click.

And then she creepy-crept down the stairs, without disturbing Grandpa or Grandma or Uncle or Aunty, into the kitchen.

It looked funny and dark in the kitchen, for the curtains were still drawn. Topsy the cat jumped off Grandma's chair and came yawning and stretching to meet her, and Milly-Molly-Mandy had to stoop down and let Topsy the cat dab her little cold nose very, very lightly against her warm cheek, for 'Good morning'.

And then Milly-Molly-Mandy went into the scullery to wash.

But when she turned on the tap she suddenly thought of the brook at the bottom of the meadow. So she just washed her hands and neck and saved her face to wash in the brook. And then she put on her frock and shoes and softly unlocked the back door, and slipped outside.

It really was a most beautiful fresh morning, full of little bird-voices; and Toby the dog was making little thumping noises in his kennel, because he had heard her and was excited to think somebody was up.

So Milly-Molly-Mandy ran and let him off the chain, but she held his collar and whispered, 'Hush, Toby! Hush, Toby!' very sternly, until they got as far as the meadow.

Then she let him go, and Toby the dog barked and capered, and Milly-Molly-Mandy, with the breeze in her hair, ran hoppity-skip down to the brook through the long grass and dewdrops that sparkled all colours in the sun.

The water looked so lovely and clear and cold, rippling over the stones, that Milly-Molly-Mandy couldn't decide all at once which was the nicest spot to wash her face in. So she was walking along beside it a little way, when suddenly whom should she see in the next field but little-friend-Susan, up early too.

'Su-san!' called Milly-Molly-Mandy.

'Milly-Molly-Mandy!' called little-friend-Susan, 'There're mushrooms in this field!'

So Milly-Molly-Mandy and Toby the dog ran and clambered through the railings into the next field. And there *were* mushrooms in that field, for Milly-Molly-Mandy nearly trod on one straight away. Only she just didn't – she picked it and ran to show it to little-friend-Susan and say, 'Fancy you being up so early, Susan!' And little-friend-Susan ran to show Milly-Molly-Mandy her three mushrooms and say, 'Fancy you being up so early, Milly-Molly-Mandy!'

Then they searched all over the field together, but they didn't find any more mushrooms. And then

'There're mushrooms in this field!'

they came to another field, and suddenly whom should they see in the middle of the other field but Billy Blunt, up early too.

'Bil-ly' called Milly-Molly-Mandy.

'Mushrooms!' called Billy Blunt.

So Milly-Molly-Mandy and little-friend-Susan and Toby the dog ran and clambered over the stile into the other field, and went to show Billy Blunt their mushrooms and say, 'Fancy you being up so early, Billy!' And Billy Blunt came to show them his two mushrooms and say, 'Fancy anybody stopping in bed!'

And then they found quite a lot of mushrooms growing together in one patch, and they all gave a gasp and a shout and set to work picking in great excitement.

When they had finished gathering whom should they see coming into the field with a basket over his arm but a shabby boy who had run in a race with Billy Blunt at a fête last Bank Holiday (and beaten him!).

He seemed to be looking for mushrooms too; and as he came near Milly-Molly-Mandy smiled at him a bit, and he smiled a bit back. And little-friend-Susan said, 'Hullo!' and he said, 'Hullo!' And Billy Blunt said, 'Plenty of mushrooms here.' And the boy said, 'Are there?'

Then Milly-Molly-Mandy said, 'Look what we've got!' And the boy looked.

And then little-friend-Susan said, 'How many've you got?' And the boy showed his basket, but there weren't many in it.

And then Billy Blunt said, 'What are you going to do with them?'

And the boy said, 'Sell them to Mr Smale the Grocer, if I can get enough. If not, we eat them, my grandad and I. Only we'd rather have the money.'

Then Milly-Molly-Mandy said, 'Let's help to get the basket full!'

So they spread about over the field and looked everywhere for mushrooms, and they really got quite a lot; but the basket wasn't full. Then Billy Blunt and Milly-Molly-Mandy and little-friend-Susan looked questioningly at each other and at their own heap of mushrooms, and then they nodded to each other and piled them all into the basket.

'My word!' said the boy, with a beaming face. 'Won't Grandad be pleased today!' Then he thanked them all very much and said good-bye and went off home.

Milly-Molly-Mandy and little-friend-Susan and Billy Blunt felt very satisfied with their morning's work. They had enjoyed it so much that they made plans to get up early another morning and go mushrooming together, with baskets – for themselves, this time.

And then they all said 'Good-bye' till they should meet again for school, and Milly-Molly-Mandy called Toby the dog, and they went off home to their breakfast.

And it wasn't until she got in that Milly-Molly-Mandy remembered she had never washed her face in the brook after all, and she had to go up and do it in a basin in the ordinary way!

2. *Milly-Molly-Mandy Has a Surprise*

Once upon a time Milly-Molly-Mandy was helping Mother to fetch some pots of jam down from the little storeroom.

Father and Mother and Grandpa and Grandma and Uncle and Aunty and Milly-Molly-Mandy between them ate quite a lot of jam, so Mother (who made all the jam) had to keep the pots upstairs because the kitchen cupboard wouldn't hold them all.

The little storeroom was up under the thatched roof, and it had a little square window very near to the floor, and the ceiling sloped away on each side so that Father or Mother or Grandpa or Grandma or Uncle or Aunty could stand upright only in the very middle of the room. (But Milly-Molly-Mandy could stand upright anywhere in it.)

When Mother and Milly-Molly-Mandy had found the jams they wanted (strawberry jam and blackberry jam and ginger jam), Mother looked round the little storeroom and said,

'It is a pity I haven't got somewhere else to keep my jam-pots!'

And Milly-Molly-Mandy said, 'Why, Mother, I think this is a very nice place for jam-pots to live in!'

And Mother said, 'Do you?'

But a few days later Father and Mother went up to the little storeroom together and took out all the jam-pots and all the shelves that held the jam-pots, and Father stood them down in the new shed he was making outside the back door, while Mother started cleaning out the little storeroom.

Milly-Molly-Mandy helped by washing the little square window – 'So that my jam-pots can see out!' Mother said.

The next day Milly-Molly-Mandy came upon

Father in the barn, mixing colour-wash in a bucket. It was a pretty colour, just like a pale new primrose, and Milly-Molly-Mandy dabbled in it with a bit of stick for a while, and then she asked what it was for.

And Father said, 'I'm going to do over the walls and ceiling of the little storeroom with it.' And then he added, 'Don't you think it will make the jam-pots feel nice and cheerful?'

And Milly-Molly-Mandy said she was sure the jam-pots would just love it! (It was such fun!)

A little while afterwards Mother sent Milly-Molly-Mandy to the village to buy a packet of green dye at Mr Smale the Grocer's shop. And then Mother dyed some old casement curtains a bright green for the little storeroom window. 'Because,' said Mother, 'the window looks so bare from outside.'

And while she was about it she said she might as well dye the coverlet on Milly-Molly-Mandy's little cot-bed (which stood in one corner of Father's and Mother's room), as the pattern had washed nearly white. So Milly-Molly-Mandy had a nice new bedspread, instead of a faded old one.

The next Saturday, when Grandpa came home from market, he brought with him in the back of the pony-trap a little chest of drawers, which he said he had 'picked up cheap'. He thought it might come in useful for keeping things in, in the little storeroom.

And Mother said, yes, it would come in very useful indeed. So (as it was rather shabby) Uncle, who had been painting the door of the new shed with apple-green paint, painted the little chest of drawers green too, so that it was a very pretty little chest of drawers indeed.

'Well,' said Uncle, 'that ought to make any jampot taste sweet!'

Milly-Molly-Mandy began to think the little storeroom would be almost too good just for jampots.

Then Aunty decided she and Uncle wanted a new mirror in their room, and she asked Mother if their little old one couldn't be stored up in the little storeroom. And when Mother said it could, Uncle said he might as well use up the last of the green paint, so that he could throw away the tin. So he painted the frame of the mirror green, and it looked a very pretty little mirror indeed.

'Jam-pots don't want to look at themselves,' said Milly-Molly-Mandy. She thought the mirror looked much too pretty for the little storeroom.

'Oh well – a mirror helps to make the room lighter,' said Mother.

Then Milly-Molly-Mandy came upon Grandma

embroidering a pretty little wool bird on either end of a strip of coarse linen. It was a robin, with a brown back and a scarlet front. Milly-Molly-Mandy thought it *was* a pretty cloth: and she wanted to know what it was for.

And Grandma said, 'I just thought it would look nice on the little chest of drawers in the little storeroom.' And then she added, 'It might amuse the jam-pots!'

And Milly-Molly-Mandy laughed, and begged Grandma to tell her what the pretty cloth really was for. But Grandma would only chuckle and say it was to amuse the jam-pots.

The next day, when Milly-Molly-Mandy came home from school, Mother said, 'Milly-Molly-Mandy, we've got the little storeroom in order again. Now, would you please run up and fetch me a pot of jam?'

Milly-Molly-Mandy said, 'Yes, Mother. What sort?'

And Father said, 'Blackberry.'

And Grandpa said, 'Marrow-ginger.'

And Grandma said, 'Red-currant.'

And Uncle said, 'Strawberry.'

And Aunty said, 'Raspberry.'

But Mother said, 'Any sort you like, Milly-Molly-Mandy!'

Milly-Molly-Mandy thought something funny must be going to happen, for Father and Mother and Grandpa and Grandma and Uncle and Aunty all looked as if they had got a laugh down inside them. But she ran upstairs to the little storeroom.

And when she opened the door – she saw –

Her own little cot-bed with the green coverlet on, just inside. And the little square window with the green curtains blowing in the wind. And a yellow pot of nasturtiums on the sill. And the little green chest of drawers with the robin cloth on it. And the little green mirror hanging on the primrose wall, with Milly-Molly-Mandy's own face reflected in it.

And then Milly-Molly-Mandy knew that the little storeroom was to be her very own little bed-

She said 'O-h-h-h!' in a very hushed voice

room, and she said 'O-h-h-h!' in a very hushed voice, as she looked all round her room.

Then suddenly she tore downstairs back into the kitchen, and just hugged Father and Mother and Grandpa and Grandma and Uncle and Aunty; and they all said she was their favourite jam-pot and pretended to eat her up!

And Milly-Molly-Mandy didn't know how to wait till bedtime, because she was so eager to go to sleep in the little room that was her Very Own!

3. Milly-Molly-Mandy Gets Up a Tree

Once upon a time Milly-Molly-Mandy saw a ladder leaning against the branch of a tree just past the duck-pond at the corner of the village.

It was a nice long ladder and a nice big branch and a nice green spreading tree, and Milly-Molly-Mandy thought how nice to climb the ladder and sit on the branch in the spreading tree and see how much she could see up there!

So she climbed the ladder very carefully, and then she sat on the branch, with the green leaves tickling her legs and flipping up and down on her hat.

It was such a nice place – she could see right down the village street as far as the crossroads (where the red bus was just passing). And she could see right up the white road, with the hedges each side, as far as the nice white cottage with the thatched roof (where she lived with Father and Mother and Grandpa and Grandma and Uncle and Aunty). And she could see at one glance the whole of the duck-pond (where three ducks were waggling their tails and making gabbly sounds in the water with their beaks).

Milly-Molly-Mandy wished she could stay up there all day, only she thought perhaps she had better be getting down now. But she just waited until a cart had passed, and then she just waited until the Grocer's boy had gone out of sight with his basket of groceries. And then she turned carefully to climb down the ladder again.

But Milly-Molly-Mandy had never noticed that the man who left the ladder there had come and fetched it while the cart was rattling past (not dreaming there was anyone up in the tree).

She only saw that the ladder was ab-so-lute-ly gone!

Milly-Molly-Mandy sat and held on and thought. It had felt so nice being up in the tree while she thought she could get down from it any minute; it was very funny, but it didn't feel a little bit nice directly she found she couldn't.

'If I shouted as loud as ever I can, somebody might hear,' thought Milly-Molly-Mandy, 'only

The ladder was ab-so-lute-ly gone!

I'd have to scream so loud they might think I was in trouble, and I'm not really. I only want to get down.'

So Milly-Molly-Mandy held on and thought some more. 'Somebody's sure to go by soon,' thought Milly-Molly-Mandy, 'and then I'll ask them please to help me down.'

So Milly-Molly-Mandy sat and tried to remember how nice the tree was before she found she couldn't get out of it. And while she was thinking that she saw a nest on a branch with a little bird peeping out of it.

'It's all right, Mrs Bird,' said Milly-Molly-Mandy. 'I won't frighten you. I'm *glad* you're here to keep me company.'

And then she saw a little red lady-bird on a leaf. 'Hullo, Mrs Lady-bird!' said Milly-Molly-Mandy. 'You don't mind being up in a tree, do you? I expect you like it quite a lot.' And somehow the tree seemed nicer again.

Presently a horse came slowly clip-clopping along from the crossroads, led by a man, and they walked down the village street; and Milly-Molly-Mandy got all ready to call out politely as soon as they came near enough. But the man turned off by the forge, and the horse clip-clopped after him, to have some new shoes put on.

Next Milly-Molly-Mandy saw Mrs Jakes, the Postman's wife, come out into her back garden and hang up a towel. Milly-Molly-Mandy waved, but Mrs Jakes didn't see her, and went in and shut the door.

Presently Milly-Molly-Mandy saw old Mr Hubble step out of the Baker's shop, and come walking along with his stick. Old Mr Hubble always walked about all day saying, 'Fine morning!' to everybody he met. But when he met Milly-Molly-Mandy he always pretended to give her a little poke with his stick, and it made Milly-Molly-Mandy feel rather shy, as she didn't know quite what to answer to that – she just used to smile a bit and run as hard as she could on her way.

So Milly-Molly-Mandy watched old Mr Hubble and his stick coming along towards her down the street, and wondered if he would see her. And when he didn't, she suddenly felt shy, thinking of his stick, and didn't want to call out as he went past (though a moment afterwards she wished she had, for she didn't *really* think he would poke her with his stick up there).

'Oh dear!' thought Milly-Molly-Mandy. 'I *must* shout out to the next person who comes by.'

The next person who came in sight was a little girl in a white muslin frock, who went into Miss

Muggins's shop. Milly-Molly-Mandy had seen her before – she had just come to live at the Big House with the iron railings, past the crossroads. Presently the little girl came out again with a little paper

bag (Milly-Molly-Mandy wondered if it held rasp-berry-drops or aniseed-balls). She was rather a long way off, but Milly-Molly-Mandy thought she must try to shout loud enough to make her hear.

But then she couldn't think what to shout! The little girl didn't look quite the sort of little girl you'd suddenly shout 'Hi!' to, and Milly-Molly-Mandy didn't want to call out 'Help!' as if she were falling, and she didn't know the little girl's name. It was really quite awkward.

And then the little girl popped something from

the paper bag into her mouth and wandered down to look at the ducks. And when she got near she suddenly saw Milly-Molly-Mandy up in the tree!

The little girl stopped and looked at Milly-Molly-Mandy, and Milly-Molly-Mandy held on and looked at the little girl. And then the little girl said, 'Can't you get down?'

And Milly-Molly-Mandy said, 'Oh, *please* will you help to get me down? I've been up here such a *long* time!'

So the little girl looked around, and then she ran back to Mr Blunt's garden and beckoned someone to the palings. And then Billy Blunt's head looked over. And then the little girl explained what was the matter. And then Billy Blunt ran out of the garden into the corn-shop. And then Mr Blunt came out of the corn-shop with a long ladder. And then he set the ladder under the tree and climbed up. And then he hoisted Milly-Molly-Mandy off the branch on to his shoulder, and brought her safely down. (And it was good to be on the ground once more!)

Milly-Molly-Mandy said, 'Thank you very much!' to Mr Blunt and Billy Blunt, and then the little girl gave her a raspberry-drop, and they talked. And then they had another raspberry-drop, and the little girl said she had a summer-house in her garden, and asked if Milly-Molly-Mandy would come and play in it with her that afternoon.

So, as soon as Milly-Molly-Mandy had finished dinner, Mother put a clean pink-and-white cotton frock on her, and she ran hoppity-skip all the way down to the village.

And Milly-Molly-Mandy felt very glad indeed that she hadn't called out sooner, or she might never have been invited to play with the little girl at the Big House with the iron railings!

4. Milly-Molly-Mandy Goes to a Concert

Once upon a time Milly-Molly-Mandy was going to a grown-up concert with Father and Mother and Grandpa and Grandma and Uncle and Aunty. (They had all got their tickets.)

It was to be held in the Village Institute at seven o'clock, and it wouldn't be over until quite nine o'clock, which was lovely and late for Milly-Molly-Mandy. But you see this wasn't like an ordinary concert, where people you didn't know sang and did things.

It was a quite extra specially important concert, for Aunty was going to play on the piano on the platform, and the young lady who helped Mrs Hubble in her Baker's shop was going to sing, and some other people whom Milly-Molly-Mandy had heard spoken of were going to do things too. So it was very exciting indeed.

Aunty had a new mauve silk scarf for her neck, and a newly trimmed hat, and her handkerchief was sprinkled with the lavender-water that Milly-Molly-Mandy had given her last Christmas.

Milly-Molly-Mandy felt so proud that it was being used for such a special occasion. (Aunty put a drop on Milly-Molly-Mandy's own handkerchief too.)

When they had all got into their best clothes and shoes, they said good-bye to Toby the dog and Topsy the cat, and started off for the village – Father and Mother and Grandpa and Grandma and Uncle and Aunty and Milly-Molly-Mandy. And they as nearly as possible forgot to take the tickets with them off the mantelpiece! But Mother remembered just in time.

There were several people already in their seats when Father and Mother and Grandpa and Grandma and Uncle and Aunty and Milly-Molly-Mandy got to the Institute. Mr and Mrs Hubble and the young lady who helped them were just in front, and Mr and Mrs Blunt and Mr and Mrs Moggs (little-friend-Susan's father and mother) were just behind (Billy Blunt and little-friend-Susan weren't there, but then they hadn't got an aunty who was going to play on the platform, so it wasn't so important for them to be up late).

The platform looked very nice, with plants in crinkly green paper. And the piano was standing there, all ready for Aunty. People were coming in very fast, and it wasn't long before the hall was full, everybody was talking and rustling programmes. Then people started clapping, and Milly-Molly-Mandy saw that some ladies and gentlemen with violins and things were going up steps on to the platform, with very solemn faces. A lady hit one or two notes on the piano, and the people with violins played a lot of funny noises without taking any notice of each other (Mother said they were 'tuning up'). And then they all started off playing properly, and the concert had begun.

Milly-Molly-Mandy did enjoy it. She clapped as hard as ever she could, and so did everybody else, when the music stopped. After that people sang one at a time, or a lot at a time, or played the piano, and one man sang a funny song (which made Milly-Molly-Mandy laugh and everybody else too).

But Milly-Molly-Mandy was longing for the time to come for Aunty to play.

She was just asking Mother in a whisper when Aunty was going to play, when she heard a queer little sound, just like a dog walking on the wooden floor. And she looked round and saw people at the back of the hall glancing down here and there, smiling and pointing.

And presently what should she feel but a cold, wet nose on her leg, and what should she see but a white, furry object coming out from under her chair.

And there was Toby the dog (without a ticket), looking just as pleased with himself as he could be for having found them!

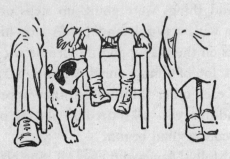

Milly-Molly-Mandy was very shocked at him, and so was Mother. She said, 'Naughty Toby!' in a whisper, and Father pushed him under the seat and made him lie down. They couldn't disturb the concert by taking him out just then.

So there Toby the dog stayed and heard the concert without a ticket; and now and then Milly-Molly-Mandy put down her hand and Toby the dog licked it and half got up to wag his tail. But Father said, 'Ssh!' so Milly-Molly-Mandy put her hand back in her lap, and Toby the dog settled down again. But they liked being near each other.

Then the time came for the young lady who helped Mrs Hubble to sing, and Aunty to play for her. So the young lady got up and dropped her handbag, and Aunty got up and dropped her music (it made Toby the dog jump!). But they were picked up again, and then Aunty and the young lady went up on to the platform.

And who *do* you think went up with them?

Why, Toby the dog! Looking just as if he thought Aunty had meant him to follow!

Everybody laughed, and Aunty pointed to Toby the dog to go down again. But Toby the dog didn't seem to understand, and he got behind the piano and wouldn't come out.

So Aunty had to play and the young lady to sing with Toby the dog peeping out now and then from behind the piano, and everybody tried not to notice him, lest it should make them laugh.

But still Aunty played beautifully and the young lady sang, and Milly-Molly-Mandy clapped as hard as she could, and so did everybody else when the song was finished. In fact, they all clapped so loud that Toby the dog gave a surprised bark, and everybody laughed again.

They had another try then to get Toby the dog off the platform, but Toby the dog wouldn't come.

Then Father said, 'Milly-Molly-Mandy, you go and see if you can get him.'

So Milly-Molly-Mandy slipped off her seat, past the people's knees, and climbed up the steps on to the platform (in front of all the audience).

And she said, 'Toby, come here!' round the corner of the piano, and Toby the dog put out his nose and sniffed her hand, and Milly-Molly-Mandy was able to catch hold of his collar and pull him out.

She walked right across the platform with Toby the dog in her arms, and everybody laughed, and somebody (I think it was the Blacksmith) called out, 'Bravo! Encore!' and clapped.

And Milly-Molly-Mandy (feeling very hot) hurried down the steps, with Toby the dog licking all over one side of her cheek and hair.

There was only a little bit of the concert to come after that, so Milly-Molly-Mandy stood at the back of the hall with Toby the dog till it was finished. Then everybody started crowding to the door. Most of them smiled at Milly-Molly-Mandy and Toby

She walked right across the platform

the dog as they stood waiting for Father and Mother and Grandpa and Grandma and Uncle and Aunty to come.

Mr Jakes the Postman, passing with Mrs Jakes, said, 'Well, well! I didn't expect to see you turning out a public character just yet awhile, young lady.' And Milly-Molly-Mandy laughed with Mr Jakes.

Then Mr Rudge, the Blacksmith, passed, and he said solemnly, 'You and Toby gave us a very fine performance indeed. If I'd known beforehand I'd have sent you up a bouquet each.' Milly-Molly-Mandy liked the Blacksmith – he was a nice man.

'Well,' said Aunty, as they all walked home together in the dark, 'I think if we'd known Toby was going to perform up on the platform tonight we'd have given him a bath and a new collar first!'

5. *Milly-Molly-Mandy Has her Photo Taken*

Once upon a time, when Milly-Molly-Mandy went down to the village with a list of things Mother wanted from the Grocer's, she saw something new in the middle of Mr Smale the Grocer's shop-window.

It was a board with some photographs of people pinned on, and underneath them was written that Mr D. Hammett would be there to take tasteful and artistic photos for one week only at prices strictly moderate.

When Milly-Molly-Mandy went up the step into

the shop (which always had such a smell of its own, a cardboardy, bacony sort of smell) she looked about, wondering where Mr D. Hammett was and what his camera was like.

She guessed he must be in the little room at the back of the shop, for there was a notice on the door, though it was too dark to read it; and through the door (which was a bit open) she could see part of what looked like a sheet hung up, with grey bulrushes painted on it.

While Mr Smale was taking her order (the raisins and baking-powder she was to bring, as Mother was wanting them, but the other things were too heavy, so Mr Smale was please to send them later) Milly-Molly-Mandy kept her eye on the door at the back of the shop. And presently it opened, and a young man with a pink face (he had just had his photo taken) hurried out of the shop; while another man with a small moustache and his hair parted in the middle said, 'Good morning to you, sir,' from the doorway.

Milly-Molly-Mandy guessed this must be Mr D. Hammett himself, but she did not stare at him.

Mr D. Hammett said, 'Good morning, young lady. Wouldn't you like to have your photo taken?'

Milly-Molly-Mandy said, 'No, thank you,' but she took one of his handbills which he gave her.

And while she was walking back along the white road with the hedges each side she read it all through.

And she found the price for one person alone was one shilling each photograph, artistically mounted. (If you wanted a group it was more money.) Milly-Molly-Mandy had exactly one shilling in her money-box, which was very funny. She had counted it only yesterday, all in pennies.

When Milly-Molly-Mandy got home to the nice white cottage with the thatched roof, she was just going to give Mother the handbill, with the raisins and baking-powder, when all of a sudden she thought she wouldn't, for she had an idea! It was a very exciting idea indeed! Milly-Molly-Mandy wondered if she could ever do it – it was such an exciting idea!

And this is what the idea was: She would have her photo taken all by herself, without telling anybody, and give it to Mother for a surprise present!

That very afternoon Milly-Molly-Mandy slipped up to her little bedroom, and brushed her hair and put on her hat and pulled up her socks and washed her hands and face and got the pennies out of her money-box. And she was just creeping downstairs when Aunty called:

'Milly-Molly-Mandy! Uncle is driving me into the town to get some material. Do you want to come too?'

Milly-Molly-Mandy didn't like to say no, because they would wonder why, as she generally liked the chance of a drive in the pony-trap to see all the shops and things. So she had to put off going to the photographer's that day.

Next day Milly-Molly-Mandy tidied up again and swung on the gate for a little while before she went down to the village, so that nobody should wonder where or why she was going.

But when she got to the village, whom should she meet but Miss Muggins's niece, Jilly. And Miss Muggins's Jilly said, 'Hullo, Milly-Molly-Mandy! Where're you going?'

Milly-Molly-Mandy didn't want to tell Miss Muggins's Jilly her secret, so they stood and talked for a bit. But Miss Muggins's Jilly didn't seem as if she would go, so at last Milly-Molly-Mandy had just to walk back home again, with her pennies still in her hand!

The next day Grandma wanted Milly-Molly-Mandy to get her some wool from Miss Muggins's shop, and Milly-Molly-Mandy thought she might perhaps manage to be photographed at the same time. So she tidied herself carefully and set off.

But as she passed the Moggs's cottage little-friend-Susan popped her head over the wall and said, 'Hullo, Milly-Molly-Mandy! Where're you going? Wait for me!' So they went on together.

When Milly-Molly-Mandy had got the wool from Miss Muggins's shop, she said, 'You'd better not wait for me, Susan – I think perhaps I'm going to the Grocer's next.'

But little-friend-Susan said, 'Oh, I don't mind waiting. You won't be long, will you?'

Milly-Molly-Mandy thought a moment. After all, little-friend-Susan was a 'best friend'. So she said in a whisper, 'Susan, if you won't say a single tiny word I'll tell you a great secret! I'm going to get my photo taken for Mother! But you're not to say a single tiny word, Susan.'

Little-friend-Susan solemnly promised not to say a single tiny word about it, and then she waited patiently while Milly-Molly-Mandy went into Mr Smale the Grocer's shop, holding her pennies very tight.

Mr D. Hammett said he was fortunately dis-engaged at that moment, so he took her straight into the back room where the bulrush sheet was hanging. Milly-Molly-Mandy gave him her handful of pennies lest she should drop them in the middle of the photographing.

And then Mr D. Hammett stood her by a little table in front of the bulrush sheet, and he took some flowers out of a vase and gave them to her to hold. (Milly-Molly-Mandy didn't much like it, because the stalks were wet!)

Then Mr D. Hammett put a black cloth over his head and moved his camera's long legs about. And then he said, 'Do you think you could manage a smile – just a very little one?' But Milly-Molly-Mandy felt as if she didn't know a bit how to smile – it all felt so solemn and queer. So Mr D. Hammett took the photo as she was.

And then he took the flowers from her hand and said that the photo would be ready on the morrow, if she would kindly call for it, and he bowed her out. And Milly-Molly-Mandy felt very glad that little-friend-Susan was outside waiting for her.

After breakfast next day Milly-Molly-Mandy said to Mother, 'Mother, would you like something nice to happen today?'

And Mother said, 'I always like something nice to happen, Milly-Molly-Mandy!'

Then Milly-Molly-Mandy said, 'I think – I'm not sure, but I *think* – something extra nice is going to happen today!' And Mother was very pleased.

When Milly-Molly-Mandy went down to the village it was too early, and the photo wasn't

'Do you think you could manage a smile?'

finished yet, but Mr D. Hammett said it would be ready that afternoon.

At dinner-time Mother said, 'Milly-Molly-Mandy, hasn't the nice thing happened yet? I'm getting so excited.'

And Milly-Molly-Mandy said, 'It's very nearly happened. I wonder if you're going to like it!' Mother was quite sure that she was; and Father and Grandpa and Grandma and Uncle and Aunty were all very curious.

That afternoon Mr D. Hammett had the photo ready for her, wrapped in paper, and Milly-Molly-Mandy ran nearly all the way home with it. (She stopped a minute at the Moggs's cottage to show it to little-friend-Susan, who thought it was lovely.)

She ran straight into the kitchen and put it in Mother's lap, on the darning-bag, and stood holding herself in very tight.

Mother said, 'Oh, Milly-Molly-Mandy! I do believe the nice thing has really happened!' She opened the paper very slowly and carefully, and took out the photograph, stuck on a beautiful card with crinkled edges.

And when Mother looked at the photograph she said: 'Why! If it isn't a picture of my little Milly-Molly-Mandy, looking as solemn as a little owl!'

And Mother and Milly-Molly-Mandy laughed

and hugged each other, while Father and Grandpa and Grandma and Uncle and Aunty all looked at the photograph in turn.

D. Hammett, Photos.

Then Mother wanted it back, and she put it on the mantelpiece where they could all see it.

And Mother thought it was a lovely surprise present, though she couldn't help laughing each time she looked at it. But that, said Mother, was only because she was so *very pleased*!

6. *Milly-Molly-Mandy Goes to the Pictures*

Once upon a time Milly-Molly-Mandy found out there was a moving-picture show every Saturday evening in the next village. (It was the young lady who helped Mrs Hubble in the Baker's shop who told her.)

Milly-Molly-Mandy told Father and Mother and Grandpa and Grandma and Uncle and Aunty directly she got home to the nice white cottage with the thatched roof. And Father and Mother and Grandpa and Grandma and Uncle and Aunty thought they might go one Saturday evening for a special treat (with Milly-Molly-Mandy of course), in the red bus that ran between their village and the next.

So one Saturday evening, early, they all put on their hats and coats and walked down through the village to the crossroads (where the red bus always stopped).

As they passed the Moggs's cottage little-friend-Susan was swinging on her swing, and Milly-Molly-Mandy waved to her and said, 'Hullo, Susan! We're going in the bus to the pictures!'

And little-friend-Susan waved back and said, 'We're going next Saturday!' So Milly-Molly-Mandy felt very glad for little-friend-Susan.

As they passed Mr Blunt's corn-shop Billy Blunt was making himself a scooter in the little garden at the side, and Milly-Molly-Mandy waved to him and said, 'Hullo, Billy! We're going in the bus to the pictures!'

And Billy Blunt looked round with a grin and said, 'I went last Saturday!' So Milly-Molly-Mandy felt very glad for Billy Blunt.

When they came to the crossroads the red bus was just in sight, and Milly-Molly-Mandy gave a little skip, because it was very exciting.

Then the red bus came close and pulled up, and they all crowded to the steps, Father and Mother and Grandpa and Grandma and Uncle and Aunty and Milly-Molly-Mandy.

But the Conductor put out his hand and said loudly. 'Only room for two!'

So they had to decide quickly who should go. Uncle and Aunty wanted Grandpa and Grandma to go, and Grandpa and Grandma wanted Father and Mother to go, and Father and Mother wanted not to go at all if they couldn't all go together.

Then Grandpa and Grandma and Uncle and Aunty said, 'Milly-Molly-Mandy will be so disappointed if she doesn't see the pictures. You take her, Father and Mother – there'll be room for her on your lap.'

Then the Conductor said, 'Hurry up, please!' (but quite kindly), so Father and Mother with Milly-Molly-Mandy hurried up into the red bus and squeezed past the other people into the two seats.

And Milly-Molly-Mandy, standing between Father's knees while he got the money out of his pocket, watched Grandpa and Grandma and Uncle and Aunty getting smaller and smaller in the distance, until she couldn't see them any more.

And Milly-Molly-Mandy felt very sorry indeed they weren't coming to the pictures too.

Then Mother said, 'Well, Milly-Molly-Mandy,

we must enjoy ourselves all we can, or Grandpa and Grandma and Uncle and Aunty will be so disappointed, because they wanted us to enjoy ourselves.'

So Milly-Molly-Mandy cheered up and began to look out of the windows, and at the other people in the bus. Mr Rudge, the Blacksmith, was sitting in the farther corner, and he smiled a nice twinkly smile at Milly-Molly-Mandy, and Milly-Molly Mandy smiled back. (They couldn't talk because the bus made such a rattly noise.)

Then they came to the next village and got down. The coloured posters outside the place where the picture show was to be looked very exciting, and Milly-Molly-Mandy did wish Grandpa and Grandma and Uncle and Aunty could see them. But she thought she would look at everything and remember very carefully, so that she could tell them all about it when they got home.

The pictures were lovely! There was a very nice man who rescued a lady just in time (Milly-Molly-Mandy knew he would); and there was a funny man who ran about a lot and fell into a dust-bin; and there was a quite close-up picture of the Prince of Wales, and someone with feathers on his hat, whom Father said was the King (the people clapped a lot, and so did Milly-Molly-Mandy).

The light went out once, and they had to turn up the gas for a little while, till they got it right; and Milly-Molly-Mandy could see where the Blacksmith was sitting. And there was a lady who looked awfully like Aunty over on the other side (only she had a little boy with her), and someone who might easily have been Grandpa. And then the light came again and they turned off the gas, and the picture went on till the end.

Milly-Molly-Mandy was sorry when it was all over. If only Grandpa and Grandma and Uncle and Aunty could have been there it would have been just perfect.

They went out quite close to the lady who looked like Aunty, and she really did look like Aunty, back view.

And then Milly-Molly-Mandy heard Father and Mother talking to someone and exclaiming; and she looked up, and there was Uncle! And Grandpa and Grandma were just behind! And the lady who looked like Aunty turned round, and it *was* Aunty! And she wasn't with the little boy at all, he belonged to somebody else.

And then Grandpa and Grandma and Uncle and Aunty explained how the lady who lived at the Big House with the iron railings near the crossroads was taking her little girl in their car to the pictures (the same little girl who helped Milly-Molly-Mandy that time when she got stuck up in a tree); and she passed while they were watching the red bus go out of sight, and offered them a lift. So they had a lovely ride, and arrived in time not to miss any of the pictures!

And when Father and Mother and Grandpa and Grandma and Uncle and Aunty and Milly-Molly-Mandy came out into the street, there was the car outside, and the lady who lived at the Big House with the iron railings smiled to them all and said, 'There's room for four going back, if you don't mind sitting close!'

Father and Mother and Grandpa and Grandma got in

And the little girl with her said, 'There's room for Milly-Molly-Mandy too, isn't there?'

So Father and Mother and Grandpa and Grandma got in, and the little girl and Milly-Molly-Mandy sat on their laps. (Uncle and Aunty went back by the red bus.)

And they had the loveliest possible ride home – just like the wind, and without any rattly noise. Milly-Molly-Mandy only wished it could have been twice as long.

So altogether it was very nice indeed that there had been only room for two on the bus going in!

7. *Milly-Molly-Mandy Goes for a Picnic*

Once upon a time, one fine morning, Milly-Molly-Mandy met little-friend-Susan. (She was eating hawthorn berries from the hedge by the roadside.)

Milly-Molly-Mandy said, 'Hullo, Susan' (eating a hawthorn berry too, in a friendly way).

And little-friend-Susan said, 'Hullo, Milly-Molly-Mandy! What do you think I'm going to do today? I'm going to take my dinner out, because Mother's busy. Look at my pockets!'

So Milly-Molly-Mandy looked, and in one of little-friend-Susan's coat pockets was a packet of bread-and-butter, and in the other was a hard-

boiled egg and an apple. Milly-Molly-Mandy thought it was a very nice thing to do indeed, and she began to feel hungry straight away.

Little-friend-Susan said, 'Couldn't you go and

see if your mother is busy? Maybe she'd like you to take your dinner out too.'

So Milly-Molly-Mandy gave a little skip, and ran back to the nice white cottage with the thatched roof to ask Mother.

And Mother looked at Milly-Molly-Mandy consideringly, and said, 'Well, maybe I can manage to be too busy to give you your dinner properly today, Milly-Molly-Mandy.'

And Milly-Molly-Mandy gave another little skip, because she was so pleased.

So Mother gave her a packet of bread-and-butter to put in one coat pocket, and a hard-boiled egg and an apple to put in the other, and told her to take her scarf and not to go in damp places and get muddy. And then Milly-Molly-Mandy gave Mother a kiss for good-bye and thank-you, and ran out to little-friend-Susan, and they started off down the road with their bulging pockets.

When they came near the village they met Billy Blunt walking along, and Milly-Molly-Mandy said, 'Hullo, Billy! Where're you going?'

And Billy Blunt said, 'Home to dinner.'

Then Milly-Molly-Mandy said, 'Susan and I are taking our dinners out because our mothers are busy. Look at our pockets!'

So Billy Blunt looked and saw the packets of

bread-and-butter in one of their coat-pockets, and the hard-boiled eggs and apples in the other, and he thought it was a very nice thing to do indeed, and he began to feel even more hungry than he did before.

Milly-Molly-Mandy said, 'Couldn't you go and see if your mother is busy? Perhaps she'd like you to take your dinner out too!'

So Billy Blunt thought a moment, and then he went in to ask his mother. And Mrs Blunt said, yes, he could if he liked; and she gave him a packet of bread-and-butter to put in one coat-pocket, and a hard-boiled egg and an apple for the other. And Billy Blunt came out and joined Milly-Molly-Mandy and little-friend-Susan, all having bulging pockets.

Then Billy Blunt said, 'Where're you planning to go?'

And Milly-Molly-Mandy and little-friend-Susan said, 'Down by the crossroads and along to the woods'.

Billy Blunt thought a moment, but he couldn't think of anywhere better, so they all started off with their bulging pockets.

As they passed the Big House with the iron railings by the crossroads the lady who lived there (her name was Mrs Green) was just getting her motor-

The little girl Jessamine said, 'Hullo, Milly-Molly-Mandy!'

car out; and the little girl (her name was Jessamine) was waiting by the gate.

Milly-Molly-Mandy smiled as they passed, and the little girl Jessamine said, 'Hullo, Milly-Molly-Mandy! Mother and I are taking our dinners out because Cook's away. Look at our basket!'

So Milly-Molly-Mandy said, 'We're taking our dinners out too! Look at our pockets!'

And then Mrs Green came up and said, 'Are we all taking our dinners out? What fun! Wouldn't you like to come with us and eat them on the Downs?'

That meant going for a ride in the motor-car, so of course Milly-Molly-Mandy and little-friend-Susan and Billy Blunt said 'Yes!' and Billy Blunt added 'Thank you!' so Milly-Molly-Mandy and little-friend-Susan added 'Thank you!' too.

So Mrs Green went back for three more mugs and some rugs and scarves and things. And then she said, 'Pile in!'

So they all piled into the car – the little girl Jessamine and Milly-Molly-Mandy and little-friend-Susan in the back (because they wanted to be together), and Billy Blunt in front beside Mrs Green (because he wanted to see how she drove) – and off they all started.

And it was fun!

Milly-Molly-Mandy hadn't been for a drive in a real car before, except once when Mrs Green had given Father and Mother and Grandpa and Grandma and herself a lift home from the pictures. Of course she had been in the red bus several times, and once the man who drove the milk-cans to the station every morning had given her a ride just for fun. But that was very rattly and different.

Mrs Green's car went so quickly, and the sun shone and the wind blew (how it did blow), and Milly-Molly-Mandy felt she wanted to shout at the top of her voice because she was so happy. Only of course she didn't – she just talked with the little girl Jessamine and little-friend-Susan about the Downs, and their favourite cakes, and that sort of thing. And Billy Blunt talked with Mrs Green (sometimes), asking what different bits of machinery were for, and watching what she did with them, and longing to have a try at driving himself.

When they came to the Downs they had a lovely time. They made a fire of sticks, not too close to a tree (for trees don't like their leaf-hair singed or their bark-clothes burned), and not too close to the bracken (for dry bracken sometimes burns more than you mean it to), but just in a nice sensible place.

Then Mrs Green made hot cocoa in a saucepan

and poured it into their mugs, and everybody brought out their packets of food. (Mrs Green and the little girl Jessamine had bread-and-butter and

hard-boiled eggs and apples too.) And Mrs Green cut up a cherry cake into big slices, and they all had to help to eat it up.

It was a lovely meal. Milly-Molly-Mandy couldn't think why anybody wanted to eat their dinner indoors.

Afterwards they carefully buried all their egg-shells and papers, and put the fire quite out, and left everything tidy, and then they set to work filling their empty pockets with acorns and conkers. But

Milly-Molly-Mandy collected fir-cones, because Father and Mother and Grandpa and Grandma and Uncle and Aunty did like a fir-cone fire; and she got her pockets and her bread-and-butter bag and her hat quite full.

When the time came to go home, Mrs Green drove them back to the village. And when Milly-Molly-Mandy and little-friend-Susan and Billy Blunt said good-bye and thank you, Mrs Green said:

'You must all come and have games with Jessamine some evening soon.'

The little girl Jessamine gave a skip, because she was pleased, and Milly-Molly-Mandy and little-friend-Susan and Billy-Blunt said 'Thank you very much!' again, though they didn't skip because they didn't feel they knew Mrs Green quite well enough just yet.

But they skipped like anything *inside*. (And after all, that's the best place to do it!)

8. Milly-Molly-Mandy Looks for a Name

Once upon a time something very surprising happened. Milly-Molly-Mandy couldn't remember anything happening before that was quite so surprising.

She came down to breakfast one morning and Aunty wasn't there, and Mother said Aunty had gone round to help Mrs Moggs.

Milly-Molly-Mandy wondered why Mrs Moggs should want helping, and Grandma said someone had come to stay at the Moggs's cottage, and little-friend-Susan would probably be wanting to tell Milly-Molly-Mandy all about it herself soon.

Milly-Molly-Mandy said, 'Is it someone Susan likes to have staying in their house?' And Mother and Grandma both said they were sure little-friend-Susan was very pleased indeed. Milly-Molly-Mandy couldn't think who it could possibly be.

But directly after breakfast little-friend-Susan came round to call for Milly-Molly-Mandy, because she couldn't wait till Milly-Molly-Mandy came to call for her on the way to school.

And little-friend-Susan was so bursting with excitement and importance that she could hardly speak at first. And then she held Milly-Molly-Mandy tight and said:

'Milly-Molly-Mandy, I've got a little baby sister come to live in our house and it's too small to have a name yet and it hasn't got any hair!'

Milly-Molly-Mandy was so surprised that she couldn't say anything at first except 'Susan!' And then she did so wish it could have been her little baby sister. But little-friend-Susan said generously, 'You can share it, Milly-Molly-Mandy, and it can be your nearly-sister, and we'll take it out riding in the pram together!'

Then Milly-Molly-Mandy asked about its name,

and little-friend-Susan said they were looking out for a nice one for it; so Milly-Molly-Mandy said she would help to look too, because they must find an extra-specially nice name.

Milly-Molly-Mandy walked all the way to school almost without saying anything, because she was so busy thinking about the little baby sister and what its name was to be.

When Miss Muggins's niece Jilly caught them up at the school gate, Milly-Molly-Mandy said, 'Susan's got a new little baby sister!'

And Miss Muggins's Jilly said, 'Has she? I've got a new kite, and it's got a tail that long!' (which was rather disappointing of Miss Muggins's Jilly).

Little-friend-Susan said, 'It hasn't got any name yet.'

And Miss Muggins's Jilly said, 'Hasn't it? My doll's name's Gladys.' But Milly-Molly-Mandy didn't like that name much.

After school they met Billy Blunt going home, and Milly-Molly-Mandy said, 'Susan's got a new little baby sister!'

And Billy Blunt said, 'I'd rather have a puppy.' (Which sounded rather queer of Billy Blunt; but anyhow, next day when Mrs Blunt sent him to the Moggs's cottage with a bag of oranges for Mrs Moggs, he bought a little pink rattle at Miss Muggins's shop and put it in the bag. And nobody knew it was from Billy Blunt till they thanked Mrs Blunt for it and she said she didn't know anything about it.)

When they passed the forge the Blacksmith was working the handle of the great bellows up and down to make the fire roar, and after watching for a minute or two Milly-Molly-Mandy couldn't help saying to him, 'Susan's got a new little baby sister!'

And the Blacksmith said, 'Well, well, well! You don't say!' and almost dropped the handle (which was very satisfactory of the Blacksmith).

Then little-friend-Susan said, 'It hasn't got a name yet!'

And the Blacksmith (whose name was Mr Thomas Rudge) said, 'Ah! Thomas is the very best name I know. If she's a young lady you call her Thomasina!'

Milly-Molly-Mandy and little-friend-Susan didn't like that name very much, but they liked the Blacksmith – his eyes were so twinkly.

When Milly-Molly-Mandy got home to the nice white cottage with the thatched roof she saw Mrs Hurley's little hand-cart just outside the gate, and Mrs Hurley standing at the side of it cutting up fish.

Mrs Hurley came round every month selling fish (the in-between times she was selling fish in other villages), and she was very nice and fat and red-cheeked, and she cleaned the fish and slapped them about on the board on top of her cart so quickly that Milly-Molly-Mandy always loved to watch her.

So now she stopped and said, 'Hullo, Mrs Hurley!'

And Mrs Hurley said, 'Well, my darlin', and I'm glad to see you!' (Mrs Hurley always called people darlin'.)

So Milly-Molly-Mandy stood and watched Mrs Hurley slap the fish about briskly as she cleaned them with her red hands (for the wind was sometimes very cold and so were the fish, though Mrs Hurley never minded). And then Milly-Molly-Mandy said, 'Little-friend-Susan's got a new little baby sister!'

And Mrs Hurley wiped her knife on a piece of newspaper and reached for another fish and said, 'You don't tell me that! Well, to be sure! That's fine, that is!'

And Milly-Molly-Mandy said, 'Yes, isn't it? And it hasn't got a name yet, and it's my nearly-sister, so I'm looking out for one. What are your children's names, Mrs Hurley?'

'What are your children's names, Mrs Hurley?'

Mrs Hurley said, 'There's Sally (she's my eldest), and Rosy, and Minty (her name's Ermyntrude), and Gerty, and Poppy, and – let me see, all the rest is boys, so that's no good to you.'

But Milly-Molly-Mandy didn't like any of those names very much. 'I thought of Mayflower, which is a princess's name in a book, but it spoils it to put Moggs after it,' said Milly-Molly-Mandy. 'It's quite difficult to find a name for a baby, isn't it, Mrs Hurley?'

But Mrs Hurley, putting the fish which Milly-Molly-Mandy's mother had bought on to a plate, said cheerfully, 'Well, then, you can be thankful it's only one, my darlin'. I had to find eleven for mine, bless their hearts!'

And then she gave Milly-Molly-Mandy a little fish just for her very own self to eat for her supper – 'to celebrate the new little friend,' Mrs Hurley said. Milly-Molly-Mandy *was* pleased!

While she was eating her little fish (nicely fried) for supper, and enjoying it very much, and Father and Mother and Grandpa and Grandma and Uncle and Aunty were eating their ordinary fish (and enjoying it too), they all talked about names.

Grandpa said, 'I guess Emily's a nice enough name for anybody.' (Emily was Grandma's name.)

But somehow Milly-Molly-Mandy didn't think it would suit the new little baby.

Grandma said, 'I used to know a little girl called Holly – she always had her dresses trimmed with red or green.' Milly-Molly-Mandy thought that was quite a nice name.

Father said, 'I prefer Polly to Holly, myself.' But Milly-Molly-Mandy didn't want the baby to have a name which really belonged to Mother.

Mother said, 'How do you like Primrose? It sounds fresh and pretty.' Milly-Molly-Mandy thought it sounded a very nice name.

Uncle said, 'What about Sarah Jane?' But Milly-Molly-Mandy didn't like that name at all.

Aunty said, 'Try Amaryllis!' But Milly-Molly-Mandy couldn't say it very easily.

So she thought over Holly and Primrose, which she liked best. And then she decided, as the baby had come in the spring-time, it had better be Primrose.

So next morning she went round earlier to the Moggs's cottage on the way to school, to ask little-friend-Susan if the baby could be named Primrose.

But what do you think? Mrs Moggs had got a name for the baby already.

And it was Doris Moggs!

And though Milly-Molly-Mandy would much, *much* rather it had been called Primrose, yet when she was allowed to see it, and it held her tightly by

one finger (with its eyes closed), she felt she didn't care a bit what it was named – it was so sweet just as it was! (And, anyhow, it was Mrs Moggs's own baby, after all!)

9. Milly-Molly-Mandy Gets Locked In

Once upon a time Milly-Molly-Mandy got locked in her little bedroom (which had been the little storeroom up under the thatched roof).

No, she hadn't been naughty or anything like that, and nobody locked her in. But the latch on the door had gone just a bit wrong, somehow, so that once or twice Milly-Molly-Mandy had had to turn the handle several times before she could open it; so Mother said perhaps she had better not close it quite, till Father found time to mend it.

But one Saturday morning, when Milly-Molly-Mandy had helped Mother with the breakfast things and Aunty with the beds, she went up to her own little room to make the bed there, and Topsy the cat ran up with her.

Now Topsy the cat just loved Milly-Molly-Mandy to make her bed on Saturday mornings.

She would jump into the middle of the mattress and crouch down; and then Milly-Molly-Mandy would pretend not to know Topsy the cat was there at all. And she would thump the pillows and roll

Topsy the cat about with them, and whisk the sheets and blankets over and pretend to try to smooth out the lump that was Topsy the cat underneath; and Topsy the cat would come crawling out,

looking very untidy, and make a dive under the next blanket. (And it took quite a long while to make that bed sometimes!)

Well, Milly-Molly-Mandy had got the bed made at last, and then she was so out of breath she backed up against the door to rest a bit, while Topsy the cat sat in the middle of the coverlet to tidy herself up.

And it wasn't until Milly-Molly-Mandy had tidied her own hair and had wrapped her duster round Topsy the cat (so as to carry them both downstairs together) that she found she couldn't open the door, which had shut with a bang when she leaned against it!

'Well!' said Milly-Molly-Mandy to Topsy the cat, 'now what are we going to do?' She put Topsy the cat down and tried the door again.

But she couldn't open it.

Then she called 'Mother!' But Mother was downstairs in the kitchen, getting bowls and baking-tins ready for making cakes (as it was Saturday morning).

Then Milly-Molly-Mandy called 'Aunty!' But Aunty was in the parlour, giving it an extra good dusting (as it wouldn't get much next day, being Sunday).

Then Milly-Molly-Mandy called 'Grandma!' But Grandma was round by the back door, sprinkling crumbs for the birds (as it was just their busy time with all the hungry baby-birds hatching out).

'Well!' said Milly-Molly-Mandy to Topsy the cat, 'this *is* a waste of a nice fine Saturday!'

She went to the little low window, but the only person she could see was Uncle, looking like a little speck at the farther end of the meadow, doing something to his chicken-houses. Father, she knew, had gone to the next village to give someone advice about a garden; and Grandpa had gone to market.

'Well!' said Milly-Molly-Mandy to Topsy the cat, 'if I'd only got legs like a grasshopper I could just jump down – but I'd rather have my own legs, anyhow!'

Then she thought if she had a long enough piece of string she could touch the ground that way, and if she dangled it someone might see from the down-stairs windows.

So she took the cord from her dressing-gown, and then she tied to it a piece of string from her coat-pocket. And a piece of mauve ribbon which Aunty had given her. And the belt from her frock. And her two boot-laces (Topsy the cat got quite interested). And then she tied her little yellow basket on the end, and dangled and swung it out of the window backward and forward in front of the scullery win-dow below.

But nobody came, and at last Milly-Molly-Mandy got tired of this and tied the end of the line on to the window-catch, and drew her head in again.

'Well!' said Milly-Molly-Mandy to Topsy the cat. 'It's a good thing I've got such a nice little bedroom to be shut up in, anyhow!' Topsy the cat just turned herself round and round on the bed and settled down for a sleep.

Then Milly-Molly-Mandy suddenly remembered her crochet work, carefully wrapped up in a hand-kerchief on her little green chest of drawers. It was to be a bonnet for Baby Moggs (little-friend-Susan's new little sister and her own nearly-sister). It was of pale pink wool, and she was making it rather big because Mother thought Baby Moggs might grow a bit before the bonnet was finished. (Milly-Molly-Mandy did hope Baby Moggs wouldn't grow too fast.)

So Milly-Molly-Mandy sat in the middle of the floor and began crocheting.

Crocheting is quite hard work when you've done only three and a half rows in all your life before, but Milly-Molly-Mandy crocheted and crocheted until she reached the end of the row; and then she turned round and crocheted and crocheted all the way back. So that was a row and a half.

Then she heard the window-catch on which her line was tied give a little click, and she jumped up and looked out to see if someone were touching her line. But nobody was about, though she called.

But it looked as if there were something in the little yellow basket, so Milly-Molly-Mandy pulled it up in a hurry. And what do you think? In the little yellow basket was a little paperful of that nice crunchy sugar which comes inside the big lumps of peel you put in cakes. (Mother had thought the basket and line was just a game of Milly-Molly-Mandy's, and she popped the sugar in for a surprise.)

'How nice!' thought Milly-Molly-Mandy, and she dropped the little yellow basket outside again (hoping something else would be put in it) and went back to her crochet-work. And she crocheted and crunched, and crunched and crocheted, until she had done four whole rows and eaten up all the paperful of sugar.

Then, after all this time, Milly-Molly-Mandy heard Mother's voice calling outside:

'Milly-Molly-Mandy!'

And when Milly-Molly-Mandy jumped up and looked out, Mother (who had come to see if there was enough rhubarb up yet to make a tart) said, 'What are you doing, dear? You ought to be outdoors!'

So Milly-Molly-Mandy was able to tell Mother all about it; and then Mother came running up to Milly-Molly-Mandy's bedroom door.

But Mother couldn't open it, though she tried hard – and neither could Aunty.

So Mother kissed Milly-Molly-Mandy through the crack, and said she must just wait till Father came home and then he would get her out. And Milly-Molly-Mandy kissed Mother back through the crack, and sat down to her crochet-work again.

Presently the line outside the window clicked at the catch again, and Milly-Molly-Mandy looked out just in time to see Mother whisking out of sight round the corner of the cottage, and there was a big red apple in the little yellow basket! So Milly-Molly-Mandy pulled it up again, and then went back and did her crocheting between big bites at the big red apple.

And she crocheted and she crocheted and she crocheted.

Just before dinner-time Father came back, and Mother took him straight up to Milly-Molly-Mandy's bedroom door, and they tinkered about with the lock for a while, rattling and clicking and tapping.

And Milly-Molly-Mandy went on crocheting.

Then Father said through the crack, 'I'll have to break the lock, Milly-Molly-Mandy, so you mustn't mind a noise!'

Milly-Molly-Mandy put her crochet-work down, and said, 'No, Father!' (It was rather exciting!)

Then Father fetched a great big hammer, and he gave some great big bangs on the lock, and the door came bursting open in a great hurry, and Father and Mother came in. (They had to stoop their heads in Milly-Molly-Mandy's room, because it was so little and sloping.)

Milly-Molly-Mandy was so pleased to see them.

She held up her crochet-work and said, 'Look! I've crocheted nine whole rows and I haven't dropped one single stitch! Don't you think it's enough now, before you start doing it different to make it fit at the back?'

And Mother said, 'That's fine, Milly-Molly-Mandy! I'll look at it directly after dinner and see, but you'd better come downstairs now.'

So Milly-Molly-Mandy came downstairs, and they all had dinner and talked about locks and about getting new ones.

And then Mother looked at Milly-Molly-Mandy's crochet-work. And it only wanted just a little more doing to it (most of which Mother showed Milly-Molly-Mandy how to do, but some she had to do herself); and quite soon the bonnet was finished, and Milly-Molly-Mandy took it round to the Moggs's cottage in tissue paper.

It just fitted Baby Moggs perfectly!

Mrs Moggs and little-friend-Susan looked at it most admiringly, and then Mrs Moggs put it on Baby Moggs's head and tied it under her soft little chin.

And it just fitted Baby Moggs perfectly!

(But, you know, as Milly-Molly-Mandy crocheted very tightly indeed – being her first try – it was a good thing she had planned to leave enough room for Baby Moggs to grow, and a very good thing she got locked in and finished it before Baby Moggs had any time to grow, for the bonnet was only just big enough.

But you can't *think* what a darling Baby Moggs looked in it!)

10. Milly-Molly-Mandy's Mother Goes Away

Once upon a time Milly-Molly-Mandy's Mother went away from the nice white cottage with the thatched roof for a whole fortnight's holiday.

Milly-Molly-Mandy's Mother hardly ever went away for holidays – in fact, Milly-Molly-Mandy could only remember her going away once before, a long time ago (and that was only for two days).

Mrs Hooker, Mother's friend in the next town, invited her. Mrs Hooker wanted to have a holiday by the sea, and she didn't want to go alone, as it isn't so much fun, so she wrote and asked Mother to come with her.

When Mother read the letter first, she said it was very kind of Mrs Hooker, but she couldn't possibly go, as she didn't see how ever Father and Grandpa and Grandma and Uncle and Aunty and Milly-Molly-Mandy would get on without her to cook dinners for them, and wash clothes for them, and see after things.

But Aunty said she could manage to do the cooking and the washing, somehow; and Grandma said she could do Aunty's sweeping and dusting; and Milly-Molly-Mandy said she would help all she knew how; and Father and Grandpa and Uncle said they wouldn't be fussy, or make any more work than they could help.

And then they all begged Mother to write to Mrs Hooker and accept. So Mother did, and she was quite excited (and so was Milly-Molly-Mandy for her!).

Then Mother bought a new hat and a blouse and a sunshade, and she packed them in her trunk with all her best things (Milly-Molly-Mandy helping).

And then she kissed Grandpa and Grandma and Uncle and Aunty good-bye, and hugged Milly-Molly-Mandy. And then Father drove her in the pony-trap to the next town to the station to meet Mrs Hooker and go with her by train to the sea. (She kissed Father good-bye at the station.)

And so Father and Grandpa and Grandma and

Uncle and Aunty and Milly-Molly-Mandy had to manage as best they could in the nice white cottage with the thatched roof for a whole fortnight without Mother. It did feel queer.

Milly-Molly-Mandy kept forgetting, and she would run in from school to tell Mother all about something, and find it was Aunty in Mother's apron bending over the kitchen stove instead of Mother herself. And Father would put his head in at the kitchen door and say, 'Polly, will you –' and then suddenly remember that 'Polly' was having a lovely holiday by the sea (Polly was Mother's other name, of course). And they felt so pleased when they remembered, but it did seem a long time to wait till she came back.

Then one day Father said, 'I've got a plan! Don't you think it would be a good idea, while Polly's away, if we were to –'

And then Father told them all his plan; and Grandpa and Grandma and Uncle and Aunty thought it was a very fine plan, and so did Milly Molly-Mandy. (But I mustn't tell you what it was, because it was to be a surprise, and you know how secrets do get about once you start telling them! But I'll just tell you this, that they made the kitchen and the scullery and the passage outside the kitchen most dreadfully untidy, so that nothing was in its proper place, and they had to have meals like picnics, only not so nice – though Milly-Molly-Mandy thought it quite fun.)

Well, they all worked awfully hard at the plan in all their spare time, and nobody really minded having things all upset, because it was such fun to think how surprised Mother would be when she came back!

Then another day Grandpa said: 'There's something I've been meaning to do for some time, to please Polly; I guess it would be a good plan to set about it now. It is –'

And then Grandpa told them all his plan; and Father and Grandma and Uncle and Aunty thought it was a very fine plan, and so did Milly-Molly-Mandy. (But I mustn't tell you what it was! – though I will just tell you this, that Grandpa was very busy digging up things in the garden and planting them again, and bringing things home in a box at the back of the pony-trap on market-day. And Milly-Molly-Mandy helped him all she could.)

Then Uncle had a plan, and Father and Grandpa and Grandma and Aunty thought it was a very fine plan, and so did Milly-Molly-Mandy. (It's a secret, remember! – but I will just tell you this, that Uncle got a lot of bits of wood and nails and a hammer, and he was very busy in the evenings after he had shut up his chickens for the night – which he called 'putting them to bed'.

Then Grandma and Aunty had a plan, and Father and Grandpa and Uncle thought it was a very fine plan, and so did Milly-Molly-Mandy. (But I can only just tell you this, that Grandma and Aunty and Milly-Molly-Mandy, who helped too, made themselves very untidy and dusty indeed, and nobody had any cakes for tea at all that week, what with Aunty being so busy and the kitchen so upset. But nobody really minded, because it was such fun to think how pleased Mother would be when she came back!)

And then the day arrived when Mother was to return home!

They had all been working so hard in the nice white cottage with the thatched roof that the two weeks had simply flown. But they had just managed to get things straight again, and Aunty had baked a cake for tea, and Milly-Molly-Mandy had put flowers in all the vases.

When Father helped Mother down from the pony-trap it almost didn't seem as if it could be Mother at first; but of course it was! – only she had on her new hat, and she was so brown with sitting on the beach, and so very pleased to be home again!

She kissed them all round and just hugged Milly-Molly-Mandy!

And then they led her indoors.

And directly Mother got inside the doorway – she saw a beautiful new passage, all clean and painted! And she was surprised!

Then she went upstairs and took off her things, and came back down into the kitchen. And directly Mother got inside the door – she saw a beautiful new kitchen, all clean and sunny, with the ceiling whitewashed and the walls freshly painted! And she was surprised!

When they had had tea (Aunty's cake was very good, though not quite like Mother's) she helped to carry the cups and plates out into the scullery. And directly Mother got through the doorway – she saw a beautiful new scullery, all clean and whitewashed! And she was surprised!

And she was surprised!

She put the cups down on the draining board, and directly she looked out of the window – she saw a beautiful new flower garden just outside, and a rustic trellis-work hiding the dust-bin! And she was surprised!

Then Mother went upstairs to unpack. And when her trunk was cleared, Grandpa carried it up to the attic and Mother went first to open the door. And directly she opened it – Mother saw a beautifully tidy, spring-cleaned attic!

And then Mother couldn't say anything, but that they were all very dear, naughty people to have worked so hard while she was being lazy! And Father and Grandpa and Grandma and Uncle and Aunty and Milly-Molly-Mandy were all very pleased, and said they liked being naughty!

Then Mother brought out the presents she had got for them. And what do you think Milly-Molly-Mandy's present was (besides some shells which Mother had picked up on the sand)?

It was a beautiful little blue dressing-gown, which Mother had sewed and sewed for her while she sat on the beach under her new sunshade with Mrs Hooker listening to the waves splashing!

Then Father and Grandpa and Grandma and Uncle and Aunty and Milly-Molly-Mandy all said Mother was very naughty to have worked when she might have been having a nice lazy time!

But Mother said *she* liked being naughty too! – and Milly-Molly-Mandy was so pleased with her new little blue dressing-gown that she couldn't help wearing it straight away!

And then Mother put on her apron and insisted on setting to work to make them something nice for supper, so that she should feel she was really at home.

For it had been a perfect holiday, said Mother, but it was really like having another one to come home again to them all at the nice white cottage with the thatched roof.

11. *Milly-Molly-Mandy Goes to the Sea*

Once upon a time – what *do* you think? – Milly-Molly-Mandy was going to be taken to the seaside!

Milly-Molly-Mandy had never seen the sea in all her life before, and ever since Mother came back from her seaside holiday with her friend Mrs Hooker, and told Milly-Molly-Mandy about the splashy waves and the sand and the little crabs, Milly-Molly-Mandy had just longed to go there herself.

Father and Mother and Grandpa and Grandma and Uncle and Aunty just longed for her to go too, because they knew she would like it so much. But they were all so busy, and then, you know, holidays cost quite a lot of money.

So Milly-Molly-Mandy played 'seaside' instead, by the little brook in the meadow, with little-friend-Susan and Billy Blunt and the shells Mother had brought home for her. (And it was a very nice game indeed, but still Milly-Molly-Mandy did wish sometimes that it could be the real sea!)

Then one day little-friend-Susan went with her mother and baby sister to stay with a relation who let lodgings by the sea. And little-friend-Susan wrote Milly-Molly-Mandy a postcard saying how lovely it was, and how she did wish Milly-Molly-Mandy was there; and Mrs Moggs wrote Mother a postcard saying couldn't some of them manage to come down just for a day excursion, one Saturday?

Father and Mother and Grandpa and Grandma and Uncle and Aunty thought something really ought to be done about that, and they talked it over, while Milly-Molly-Mandy listened with all her ears.

But Father said he couldn't go, because he had to get his potatoes up; Mother said she couldn't go, because it was baking day, and, besides, she had just had a lovely seaside holiday; Grandpa said he couldn't go, because it was market-day; Grandma said she wasn't really very fond of train journeys; Uncle said he oughtn't to leave his cows and chickens.

But then they all said Aunty could quite well leave the sweeping and dusting for that one day.

So Aunty only said it seemed too bad that she should have all the fun. And then she and Milly-Molly-Mandy hugged each other, because it was so very exciting.

Milly-Molly-Mandy ran off to tell Billy Blunt at once, because she felt she would burst if she didn't

95

tell someone. And Billy Blunt did wish he could be going too, but his father and mother were always busy.

Milly-Molly-Mandy told Aunty, and Aunty said, 'Tell Billy Blunt to ask his mother to let him come with us, and I'll see after him!'

So Billy Blunt did, and Mrs Blunt said it was very kind of Aunty and she'd be glad to let him go.

Milly-Molly-Mandy hoppity-skipped like anything, because she was so very pleased; and Billy Blunt was very pleased too, though he didn't hoppity skip, because he always thought he was too old for such doings (but he wasn't really!).

So now they were able to plan together for Saturday, which made it much more fun.

Mother had an old bathing-dress which she cut down to fit Milly-Molly-Mandy, and the bits over she made into a flower for the shoulder (and it looked a very smart bathing-dress indeed). Billy Blunt borrowed a swimming-suit from another boy at school (but it hadn't any flower on the shoulder, of course not!).

Then Billy Blunt said to Milly-Molly-Mandy, 'If you've got swimming-suits you ought to swim. We'd better practise.'

But Milly-Molly-Mandy said, 'We haven't got enough water.'

Billy Blunt said, 'Practise in air, then – better than nothing.'

So they fetched two old boxes from the barn out into the yard, and then lay on them (on their fronts) and spread out their arms and kicked with their legs just as if they were swimming. And when Uncle came along to fetch a wheelbarrow he said it really made him feel quite cool to see them!

He showed them how to turn their hands properly, and kept calling out, 'Steady! steady! Not so fast!' as he watched them.

And then Uncle lay on his front on the box and showed them how (and he looked so funny!), and then they tried again, and Uncle said it was better that time.

So they practised until they were quite out of breath. And then they pretended to dive off the boxes, and they splashed and swallowed mouthfuls of air and swam races to the gate and shivered and dried themselves with old sacks – and it was almost as much fun as if it were real water!

Well, Saturday came at last, and Aunty and Milly-Molly-Mandy met Billy Blunt at nine o'clock by the crossroads. And then they went in the red bus to the station in the next town. And then they went in the train, *rumpty-te-tump*, *rumpty-te-tump*, all the way down to the sea.

And you can't imagine how exciting it was, when they got out at last, to walk down a road knowing they would see the real sea at the bottom! Milly-Molly-Mandy got so excited that she didn't want to look till they were up quite close.

So Billy Blunt (who had seen it once before) pulled her along right on to the edge of the sand, and then he said suddenly, 'Now look!'

And Milly-Molly-Mandy looked.

And there was the sea, all jumping with sparkles in the sunshine, as far as ever you could see. And

little-friend-Susan, with bare legs and frock tucked up, came tearing over the sand to meet them from where Mrs Moggs and Baby Moggs were sitting by a wooden breakwater.

Wasn't it fun!

They took off their shoes and their socks and their hats, and they wanted to take off their clothes and bathe, but Aunty said they must have dinner first. So they sat round and ate sandwiches and cake and fruit which Aunty had brought in a basket. And the Moggs's had theirs too out of a basket.

Then they played in the sand with Baby Moggs (who liked having her legs buried), and paddled a bit and found crabs (they didn't take them away from the water, though).

And then Aunty and Mrs Moggs said they might bathe now if they wanted to. So (as it was a very quiet sort of beach) Milly-Molly-Mandy undressed behind Aunty, and little-friend-Susan undressed behind Mrs Moggs, and Billy Blunt undressed behind the breakwater.

And then they ran right into the water in their bathing-dresses. (And little-friend-Susan thought Milly-Molly-Mandy's bathing-dress *was* smart, with the flower on the shoulder!)

But, dear me! water-swimming feels so different

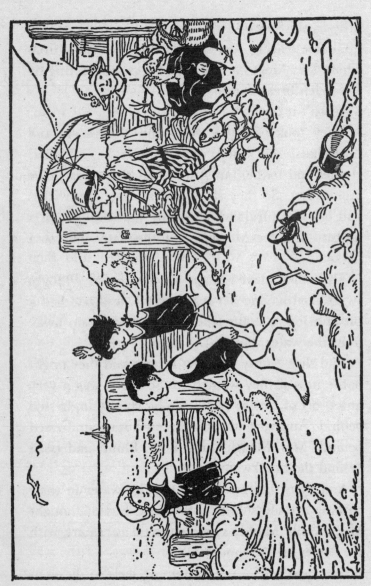

They ran right into the water in their bathing-dresses

from land-swimming, and Milly-Molly-Mandy couldn't manage at all well with the little waves splashing at her all the time. Billy Blunt swished about in the water with a very grim face, and looked exactly as if he were swimming; but when Milly-Molly-Mandy asked him, he said, 'No! my arms swim, but my legs only walk!'

It was queer, for it had seemed quite easy in the barnyard.

But they went on pretending and pretending to swim until Aunty called them out. And then they dried themselves with towels and got into their clothes again; and Billy Blunt said, well, anyhow, he supposed they were just that much nearer swimming properly than they were before; and Milly-Molly-Mandy said she supposed next time they might p'r'aps be able to lift their feet off the ground for a minute at any rate; and little-friend-Susan said she was sure she had swallowed a shrimp! (But that was only her fun!)

Then they played and explored among the rock-pools and had tea on the sand. And after tea Mrs Moggs and Baby Moggs and little-friend-Susan walked with them back to the station; and Aunty and Milly-Molly-Mandy and Billy Blunt went in the train, *rumpty-te-tump*, *rumpty-te-tump*, all the way home again.

And Milly-Molly-Mandy was so sleepy when she got to the nice white cottage with the thatched roof that she had only just time to kiss Father and Mother and Grandpa and Grandma and Uncle and Aunty good night and get into bed before she fell fast asleep.

12. *Milly-Molly-Mandy Finds a Nest*

Once upon a time, one warm summer morning, Uncle came quickly in at the back door of the nice white cottage with the thatched roof and shouted from the kitchen, 'Milly-Molly-Mandy!'

Milly-Molly-Mandy, who was just coming downstairs carrying a big bundle of washing for Mother, called back, 'Yes, Uncle?'

'Hi! quick!' said Uncle, and went outside the back door again.

Milly-Molly-Mandy couldn't think what Uncle wanted with her, but it had such an exciting sound she dropped the big bundle on the stairs in a hurry and ran down to the passage. But when she got to the passage she thought she ought not to leave the big bundle on the stairs, lest someone trip over it in the shadow; so she ran back again in a hurry and fetched the big bundle down, and ran along to the kitchen with it. But she was in such a hurry she dropped some things out of the big bundle and had to run back again and pick them up.

But at last she got them all on to the kitchen table, and then she ran out of the back door and said, 'Yes, Uncle? What is it, Uncle?'

Uncle was just going through the meadow gate, with some boards under one arm and the tool-box on the other. He beckoned to Milly-Molly-Mandy with his head (which was the only thing he had loose to do it with), so Milly-Molly-Mandy ran after him down the garden path to the meadow.

'Yes, Uncle?' said Milly-Molly-Mandy.

'Milly-Molly-Mandy,' said Uncle, striding over the grass with his boards and tool-box, 'I've found a nest.'

'What sort of a nest?' said Milly-Molly-Mandy, hoppity-skipping a bit to keep up with him.

'Milly-Molly-Mandy,' said Uncle, 'I rather think it's a Milly-Molly-Mandy nest.'

Milly-Molly-Mandy stopped and stared at Uncle,

but he strode on with his boards and tool-box as if nothing had happened.

Then Milly-Molly-Mandy began jumping up and down in a great hurry and said, 'What's a Milly-Molly-Mandy nest, Uncle? What's it like, Uncle? Where is it, Uncle? DO-O tell me!'

'Well,' said Uncle, 'you ought to know what a Milly-Molly-Mandy nest is, being a Milly-Molly-Mandy yourself. It's up in the big old oak-tree at the bottom of the meadow.'

So Milly-Molly-Mandy tore off to the big old oak-tree at the bottom of the meadow, but she couldn't see any sort of a nest there, only Uncle's ladder leaning against the tree.

Uncle put the boards and tool-box carefully down on the ground, then he settled the ladder against the big old oak-tree, then he picked up Milly-Molly-Mandy and carried her up the ladder and sat her on a nice safe branch.

And then Milly-Molly-Mandy saw there was a big hollow in the big old oak-tree (which was a very big old oak-tree indeed). And it was such a big hollow that Uncle could get right inside it himself and leave quite a lot of room over.

'Now, Milly-Molly-Mandy,' said Uncle, 'you can perch on that branch and chirp a bit while I put your nest in order.'

Then Uncle went down the ladder and brought up some of the boards and the tool-box, which he hung by its handle on a sticking-out bit of branch. And Milly-Molly-Mandy watched while Uncle measured off boards and sawed them and fitted them and hammered nails into them, until he had made a beautiful flat floor in the hollow in the big old oak-tree, so that it looked like the nicest little fairy-tale room you ever saw!

Then he hoisted Milly-Molly-Mandy off the branch, where she had been chirping with excitement like the biggest sparrow you ever saw (only that you never saw a sparrow in a pink-and-white striped cotton frock), and heaved her up into the hollow.

And Milly-Molly-Mandy stood on the beautiful flat floor and touched the funny brown walls of the big old oak-tree's inside, and looked out of the opening on to the grass down below, and thought a Milly-Molly-Mandy nest was the very nicest and excitingest place to be in in the whole wide world!

Just then whom should she see wandering along the road at the end of the meadow but little-friend-Susan!

'Susan!' called Milly-Molly-Mandy as loud as ever she could, waving her arms as hard as ever she could. And little-friend-Susan peeped over the hedge.

At first she didn't see Milly-Molly-Mandy up in her nest, and then she did, and she jumped up and down and waved; and Milly-Molly-Mandy beckoned, and little-friend-Susan ran to the meadow-

gate and couldn't get it open because she was in such a hurry, and tried to get through and couldn't because she was too big, and began to climb over and couldn't because it was rather high. So at last she squeezed round the side of the gate-post through a little gap in the hedge and came racing across the meadow to the big old oak-tree, and Uncle helped her up.

And then Milly-Molly-Mandy and little-friend-Susan sat and hugged themselves together, up in the Milly-Molly-Mandy nest.

Just then Father came by the big old oak-tree,

and when he saw what was going on he went and got a rope and threw up one end to Milly-Molly-Mandy. And then Father tied an empty wooden box to the other end, and Milly-Molly-Mandy pulled it up and untied it and set it in the middle of the floor like a little table.

Then Mother, who had been watching from the gate of the nice white cottage with the thatched roof, came and tied an old rug to the end of the rope, and little-friend-Susan pulled it up and spread it on the floor like a carpet.

Then Grandpa came along, and he tied some fine ripe plums in a basket to the end of the rope, and Milly-Molly-Mandy pulled them up and set them on the little table.

Then Grandma came across the meadow bringing some old cushions, and she tied them to the end of the rope, and little-friend-Susan pulled them up and arranged them on the carpet.

Then Aunty came along, and she tied a little flower vase on the end of a rope, and Milly-Molly-Mandy pulled it up and set it in the middle of the table. And now the Milly-Molly-Mandy nest was properly furnished, and Milly-Molly-Mandy was in such a hurry to get Billy Blunt to come to see it that she could hardly get down from it quickly enough.

Up in the Milly-Molly-Mandy nest

Mother said, 'You may ask little-friend-Susan and Billy Blunt to tea up there if you like, Milly Molly-Mandy.'

So Milly-Molly-Mandy and little-friend-Susan ran off straight away, hoppity-skip, to the Moggs's cottage (for little-friend-Susan to ask Mrs Moggs's permission), and to the village to Mr Blunt's corn-shop (to ask Billy Blunt), while Uncle fixed steps up the big old oak-tree, so that they could climb easily to the nest.

And at five o'clock that very afternoon Milly-Molly-Mandy and little-friend-Susan and Billy Blunt were sitting drinking milk from three little mugs and eating slices of bread-and-jam and gin-gerbread from three little plates, and feeling just as excited and comfortable and happy as ever they could be, up in the Milly-Molly-Mandy nest!

13. Milly-Molly-Mandy Has Friends

Once upon a time Milly-Molly-Mandy heard the Postman's knock on the door, and when she ran to look in the letterbox there was a letter for Milly-Molly-Mandy herself!

It looked rather the same kind of writing as Milly-Molly-Mandy's own, and Milly-Molly-Mandy couldn't think whom it was from. She ran to Mother who was ironing in the kitchen, and Mother looked on while Milly-Molly-Mandy tore open the envelope.

And when she pulled out the letter, two little paper girls fell out and fluttered to the floor. And Milly-Molly-Mandy said excitedly, 'Oh, I know! – it's from Milly-next-door-to-Mrs Hooker!'

Mother remembered Milly-Molly-Mandy telling her about when she went to stay with Mrs Hooker

(the old friend of Mother's in the next town), and how a little girl, Milly-next-door, had come in to play, and they had painted and cut out paper dolls together from a fashion book.

'You had better read what the letter says,' said Mother.

So Milly-Molly-Mandy set the two little paper girls up on the ironing-board and opened the letter. And this is what the letter said:

DEAR MILLY-MOLLY-MANDY,

I am sending you some paper dolls. I hope you will like them. I am coming to see you one day. Father says he will bring me when he comes to buy chickens from your uncle. I hope you will write to me. With love from

MILLY

Milly-Molly-Mandy was pleased!

Mother said, 'You must write and tell Milly-next-door to get her father to bring her over to tea with you.'

So Milly-Molly-Mandy wrote a letter to Milly-next-door, on her best fancy notepaper, and posted it herself.

Next Saturday Uncle said Mr Short was coming over to fetch some chickens that afternoon. (Mr Short was Milly-next-door's father.) So when Mother baked the cakes, which she always did on a

Saturday morning, she made a little cherry cake specially for Milly-Molly-Mandy and Milly-next-door.

And when the Muffin-man came past with his bell on the way down to the village Mother sent Milly-Molly-Mandy out to stop him. And Milly-Molly-Mandy ran and said, 'Please, we want some muffins. I've got a little friend coming to tea with me!'

So the Muffin-man came hurrying round to the back door and took the tray of muffins off his head and lifted the green baize cloth off the top, and then the nice white cloth which was underneath it. And Mother bought some muffins, while Milly-Molly-Mandy looked at the Muffin-man's bell, and rang it just a bit (it was quite heavy).

And when little-friend-Susan came along the road outside the nice white cottage with the thatched roof, to see if Milly-Molly-Mandy were coming out to play, Mother asked Milly-Molly-Mandy if she wouldn't like to invite little-friend-Susan to meet Milly-next-door.

So Milly-Molly-Mandy ran hoppity-skipping out and said to little-friend-Susan, 'Mother says will you come to tea to-day? Milly-next-door is coming!'

So little-friend-Susan ran hoppity-skipping home down the road to ask her mother; and then she ran hoppity-skipping back to Milly-Molly-Mandy and said, 'Mother says thank you very much. I'd love to come!'

That afternoon Milly-Molly-Mandy was very busy. She tidied her little bedroom, and she brushed Toby the dog and Topsy the cat as long as they would let her, and she helped to lay the table with cups and saucers and plates, and fetched a pot of strawberry jam and a pot of honey from the storeroom (outside the back door), and picked chrysanthemums for the vase in the centre of the table.

And then little-friend-Susan came in (in her Sunday frock), and she helped Milly-Molly-Mandy to arrange her dolls.

And then there was a sound of voices outside, and they looked out of the window and saw Uncle talking to Mr Short and Milly-next-door, so Mother and Milly-Molly-Mandy went out and brought Milly-next-door in, while Uncle and Mr Short went off together to the chicken enclosure.

Milly-Molly-Mandy was very glad she had a nice little bedroom of her own now to take her friends up to. Milly-next-door thought it was very pretty indeed, and she loved the robin cloth on the little green chest of drawers.

When they came downstairs again Mother had

lighted the lamp, and Aunty had drawn the curtains, and Grandma was beginning to toast the muffins before the blazing fire. Milly-Molly-Mandy and Milly-next-door and little-friend-Susan all said they would do it for Grandma.

So they sat in a row before the blazing fire and toasted muffins on forks, and little-friend-Susan and Milly-next-door quite got over feeling shy with each other, and they talked about school and paper dolls and all sorts of things. And as they toasted the muffins Grandma buttered them and stood them in the muffin dish on the stove to keep hot.

Just then there came a knock on the back door, and when Mother opened it there was Billy Blunt with a note from Mrs Blunt. (It was a recipe for ginger biscuits which Mother wanted.)

So Mother thanked Billy Blunt and said, 'You're just in time to have tea with us!'

Billy Blunt said, 'I've just had tea, really.'

But he grinned and looked quite pleased when Mother said, 'Well, come in and have another!' And he came in, and Milly-Molly-Mandy gave him her fork and he toasted muffins, while Milly-Molly-Mandy helped Grandma to butter them.

And what with the hot muffins, and the cherry cake, and the ordinary cake, and the big dish of strawberry jam, and the honey, and the new brown

'You're just in time to have tea with us!'

loaf and the white loaf, the kitchen began to smell very nice indeed.

And when Father came in from the garden, and Grandpa came in from the stable, and Uncle and Mr Short came in from the chicken enclosure, they felt very ready indeed for their tea.

Milly-Molly-Mandy and Milly-next-door and little-friend-Susan and Billy Blunt had a low table all to themselves, with the cherry cake in the middle, which Milly-Molly-Mandy cut, and the grown-ups sat round the big table. (Toby the dog and Topsy the cat liked to be by the little table best.)

And then everybody talked and laughed and ate, and the fire blazed and crackled. And every single one of the toasted muffins was eaten up. (Toby the dog got the last half muffin, but Topsy the cat would only eat cherry cake with the cherries picked out.)

As soon as everyone had finished Mr Short and Milly-next-door had to go, as the last bus left the village at a quarter past six in winter-time. So they said good-bye to Father and Mother and Grandpa and Grandma and Uncle and Aunty and Milly-Molly-Mandy and little-friend-Susan and Billy Blunt, and hoped Milly-Molly-Mandy would come to see them next time she came to stay with Mrs Hooker.

And then Mr Short and Milly-next-door went

out into the dark with two sleepy chickens in a basket (who were going to live in Mr Short's back garden now).

When they were gone there was quite a lot of washing up to be done, and Mother and Aunty began clearing the table. So little-friend-Susan said please might she stay and help. Billy Blunt didn't say anything at all, but he started putting the crumby plates together, and Milly-Molly-Mandy collected the cups and saucers.

So everybody set to work, and they had a regular clearing-up party all to themselves, each one seeing how quick and tidy they could be. Mother washed up in a big bowl of steamy water; Aunty and little-friend-Susan dried with tea-cloths; and Milly-Molly-Mandy and Billy Blunt ran backward and forward between scullery and kitchen, putting the china away in the cupboard and the spoons and knives in the basket, and Toby the dog ran backward and forward with them, and got quite excited (he thought it was some sort of a new game!).

Grandma sat knitting by the fire with Topsy the cat on her lap, because, she said, they were better out of the way with all those busy, bustling people about.

Very soon indeed everything was done, and Mother took off her apron and thanked all her helpers. And then Mr Moggs came to fetch little-friend-Susan home.

And after Milly-Molly-Mandy had seen them off down the path (Billy Blunt with them), she came back and stood in the middle of the tidy kitchen and thought how VERY nice it was to have real friends to come visiting!

Bright and shiny and sizzling with fun stuff . . .

puffin.co.uk

WEB FUN

UNIQUE and exclusive digital content!
Podcasts, photos, Q&A, Day in the Life of, interviews
and much more, from Eoin Colfer, Cathy Cassidy,
Allan Ahlberg and Meg Rosoff to Lynley Dodd!

WEB NEWS

The **Puffin Blog** is packed with posts and photos from
Puffin HQ and special guest bloggers. You can also sign up
to our monthly newsletter **Puffin Beak Speak**

WEB CHAT

Discover something new EVERY month –
books, competitions and treats galore

WEBBED FEET

(Puffins have funny little feet and
brightly coloured beaks)

Point your mouse our way today!

It all started with a Scarecrow.

Puffin is seventy years old.
Sounds ancient, doesn't it? But Puffin has never been
so lively. We're always on the lookout for the next big
idea, which is how it began all those years ago.

Penguin Books was a big idea from the mind of
a man called Allen Lane, who in 1935 invented
the quality paperback and changed the world.
**And from great Penguins, great Puffins grew,
changing the face of children's books forever.**

The first four Puffin Picture Books were hatched in 1940 and the
first Puffin story book featured a man with broomstick arms called
Worzel Gummidge. In 1967 Kaye Webb, Puffin Editor, started the
Puffin Club, promising to **'make children into readers'**.
She kept that promise and over 200,000 children became
devoted Puffineers through their quarterly instalments of
Puffin Post, which is now back for a new generation.

Many years from now, we hope you'll look back and
remember Puffin with a smile. **No matter what your age
or what you're into, there's a Puffin for everyone.**
The possibilities are endless, but one thing is for sure:
whether it's a picture book or a paperback, a sticker book
or a hardback, **if it's got that little Puffin
on it – it's bound to be good.**